THE MAD DASH

THE MAD DASH

David Aretha

TWISTED KEY
p u b l i s h i n g

2017

First Printing: 2017

ISBN 978-1-947744-09-7

Twisted Key Publishing, LLC
405 Waltham Street Suite 116
Lexington, MA 02421

www.twistedkeypublishing.com

Ordering Information:
Special discounts are available on quantity purchases by corporations, associations, educators, and others. For details, contact the publisher at the above listed address.

U.S. trade bookstores and wholesalers: Please contact Twisted Key Publishing, LLC by email twistedkeypublishing@gmail.com.

To all the young ballplayers who love the game as much as I do.

Contents

Chapter 1
Ya Gotta Believe

Patrick Quinn, the ol' left-hander, toed the rubber and stared me down. Now pushing 40, graying at the temples, Quinn had nothing left but guile and guts. I was ready for him.

I tapped my bat twice on the plate and focused on his next delivery. I leaned in, waiting…waiting.

This was my final at-bat, my last shot. *Relax*, a part of me said, *go with the pitch*. But my other self wanted to blast the daylights out of the ball. I recalled Babe Ruth's 714th and last home run, a 500-foot monster that roared out of Forbes Field. "Boy," bellowed the Babe, "that last one felt good." And for a brief instant, I thought I heard broadcaster Russ Hodges after Bobby Thomson's "Shot Heard 'Round the World" in 1951: "The Giants win the pennant! The Giants win the pennant! And they're going crazy! They're going crazy! Oh-ho!"

Finally, Quinn wound, kicked, and fired. With his face distorted in concentration, he unleashed his best effort. Like slugger Ted Williams had preached, I looked for the spin on the ball. But it didn't spin. It didn't tumble. It wasn't a curve or slider, cutter or change, splitter of knuckler. This pitch came in fat. Straight down Main Street. Room service. Right in my wheelhouse. Bells and whistles went off in my head. I went for the fences like the great Babe Ruth...and blooped a pop-up right to the pitcher.

"Arrgh!" I grunted in disgust.

"Don't sweat it, Jake," said Coach Quinn as my hit plopped like a dead bird into his mitt. "It's the first practice of the year."

He smiled and addressed my teammates in the field. "Bring it in, guys!" And with that, the team known as Morey's Funeral Home trotted toward the bench.

Yes, my team is named after an undertaker's business establishment. But that's how it goes in the Little League circuit in Hickory Oak, Michigan. Any small company can get their name slapped on a team's jerseys as long as they write a check for $300. "It could be worse," my mom had joked. "The Princess School for Ballet is looking to make a name for itself." Personally, I don't mind the funeral bit. It lends itself to good headlines:

"Morey's Sends O'Sullivan's to the Grave"
"Morey's Puts the 'Fun' in Funeral"
"Morey's: Can You Dig It?"

Anyway, this day—the first Saturday of April—
was more a day of rebirth. After five brutal months of
Michigan winter—cold, clouds, and dirty snow—
spring was coming alive. Our town's famous oak trees,
as well as maple and magnolia, were budding. A sheen
of baby grass covered the outfield, and a warm breeze
fluttered across the diamond. We felt energized.

"It's a beautiful day for baseball," beamed Gary,
our team's hyper-enthusiastic baseball junkie. "Let's
play two more hours!"

"That's not what he meant," retorted Marty, our
solemn-faced teammate who spoke in brief sentences
in a dour tone. "He meant let's play two games."

"I know what Ernie Banks meant!" Gary retorted.
"What do you think I am, a moron? I was
paraphrasing! Improvising!"

"Gary, guys, gather up," Coach said. "Everyone in
the dugout."

Our "dugout" wasn't really *dug out*, like in the big
leagues. It was just a bench behind a fence, but it did
have a special feature: a tin roof. Pretty classy, huh?
The only drawback was the occasional pop-up that

landed on it, which can only be compared to cymbals crashing against your head.

But we liked our field, which my friend Riley called a kid-sized Field of Dreams. The infield featured manicured grass with a strip of dirt leading from the mound to home plate, just like at Comerica Park (home of my Detroit Tigers!). Center field and right field were more than 200 feet away—unreachable for even the strongest 10-year-old sluggers. But left field was a tantalizing 175 feet. The chain-link fence in left soared 12 feet high, giving us our very own "Green Monster."

Our ball field rested in humble Hickory Park, which was nestled in a quiet, pleasant neighborhood— much like Wrigley Field in Chicago. Small brick houses with lots of big trees surrounded the park, which we called The Hick. I'll never forget the sounds of the season: the rustling of leaves mixing with ball field chatter. Sweet memories....

I don't have any siblings, so my teammates were kind of like my brothers and sister. (Yes, there's a girl on my team. I'll get to her later.) Not only did we all hail from the same school, Hickory Oak Elementary, but most of us had been on the same Little League team since first grade. We've always been sponsored by Morey's, which has followed us around like the Grim Reaper.

Our teams have been consistently lousy. The coaches didn't keep score in first grade (thank goodness!), and the following years we stumbled in with records of 5-9 and 4-10. Highlights included snack time, cap flipping, fence climbing, and bench parents shouting, "Get down from there and cheer on your teammates!" Pathetic baby stuff.

But this year was different. We were fourth-graders, 10 years old—double-digit maturity. Even at our first practice, I witnessed commitment never before seen by the boys of Morey's. Much of the turnaround was due to our new head coach.

Our previous coaches were moms and dads whose only skill was filling out the lineup cards so randomly that no one could possibly complain of unfair treatment. Coach Quinn, on the other hand, was the real deal. He had played baseball in *college*, starting at second base for the Central Michigan University Chippewas. As Jeffrey's dad, he had always wanted to coach us but was too busy making obscene amounts of money in real estate. This year he made time for us, and I for one was eternally grateful.

"Okay, guys, listen up," Coach said. Mr. Quinn had a perpetually smiley face. He effused enthusiasm, and he always seemed to be bopping to some beat—as if an iPod had been surgically implanted in his brain. His positive vibe energized the whole team.

All 10 of us grabbed some bench: Jeffrey, Riley, Jackson, Evan, Gary, Gus, Marty, Tashia, Rupa, and Jacob (me!). We listened up.

"I think we're going to have a great year this season, guys," Coach said.

"Oh yeah, right," quipped Tashia.

"I'm not talking about wins and losses," Coach said. "I'm talking about having fun with your teammates. Learning new skills. Enjoying the thrill of laying down a perfect bunt or turning the double play."

"Like that'll happen," interrupted Riley.

"Hey!" Coach shot back. "Riley. Look at me. I want every one of you to look me in the eye."

That caught my attention, since my dad was notorious for looking in the clouds or at the ground when he talked.

"The only way we're going to be successful this year is if we believe in ourselves—and our teammates," Coach said. "We might not be the New York Yankees, but all of you have unique skills that can help us win games. Tashia, I like how you stay down on those groundballs. Rupa? Where's Rupa."

Rupa was easy to miss. He had a severe speech impediment—so bad that he was afraid to talk, or even interact with anyone. A smaller kid, he usually melted into the background. He also was the worst player on the team, which is why Coach was calling him out for praise.

"Rupa, in baserunning drills, you were turning the corners like Bryce Harper. You were awesome, buddy!"

Rupa mustered a rare, brief smile.

"Maybe we can be like the Worst to First Twins of '87," offered Gary.

"Or the Miracle Mets of '69," I added.

"There you go, guys," said Coach. "Ya Gotta Believe!"

"Actually," interjected Gary, "that was the slogan of the '73 Mets."

"Well, we'll make it Morey's motto," Coach said. "On the count of three, Ya gotta believe. One…two…three…"

"Ya gotta believe!"

"All right," Coach said. "Next practice, Tuesday at 5:30. Eat your Wheaties!"

We all dispersed, feeling that this year was going to be a whole new ballgame. I quickly packed my equipment bag and trotted toward my dad, who was waiting near the backstop.

"Jacob," Coach said in a subdued tone. I stopped in my tracks and turned around.

"I need you to be a leader out there," Coach said.

I stared back and eventually nodded. No one had ever said anything like that to me before.

"That was a nice compliment," said my dad, putting his hand on my shoulder.

"Yeah," I said, still perplexed. "Do they have captains in Little League?"

"No," Dad said with a laugh, even though I didn't think it was a dumb question. "But you can be *like* a captain by how you act and play."

"Yeah…. Are you going to coach at all this year?"

"Well, Mr. Majus is going to help Coach Quinn. But I'll be the scorekeeper again."

Mr. Majus, a quiet old man with a big gut, had been our third base coach the previous two years. He was Gus's stepmother's father. Mr. Majus actually made it the major leagues back in 1967, but you won't find his name on baseball-reference.com. Though he played with the Cleveland Indians, he never got into a game.

Gus said that in one Indians game, Mr. Majus entered the on-deck circle as a pinch hitter in the ninth inning. But the batter ahead of him grounded into a game-ending double play, killing his big-league dream.

Now, his only tie to the game is hitting us balls in practice and coaching third base. He never gives us any advice or says hardly anything. I think it's all pretty sad, to tell you the truth.

While Coach Quinn and Jeffrey loaded their BMW X3, I slunk into Dad's '05 Chevy Malibu. "What do I need a new car for?" Dad always asks. "It gets you from point A to point B, doesn't it?"

When my dad, Douglas Vehousky, was a kid, he idolized Tigers pitcher Mark Fidrych. They called Fidrych "The Bird" because his curly blond hair made him look like Big Bird on *Sesame Street.* Fidrych electrified Tiger Stadium as a rookie in 1976. Like my dad, he was also tight with the buck. In fact, he used to fish for dimes in payphone coin returns.

"That's because he made only $16,000 as a rookie," Dad said. "Can you believe that?"

My dad knows a lot about baseball's past—and history in general. That's what he teaches at Schoolcraft College. Dad looks like a quirky professor, with circle-frame glasses and long sideburns. He seems to specialize in the history of misery: famines, plagues, economic catastrophes. He likes to talk about suffering on a grand scale ("Did you know that 75 million people died from the Black Death in the 1340s?") in order to make me "appreciate" what I have. But his history lessons usually bring me down. Moreover, on a teacher's salary, he can't afford a BMW X3.

We live in a two-bedroom brick ranch house on Ogleby Street. It's not big, but I can play baseball in the basement with a Wiffle bat and a tennis ball, spanking liners off the cement walls. My mom sews dresses for money and decorates nicely despite Dad's tight budget.

Though recently traumatized by turning 45, Mom (Bridget) has the spirit of a kindergartner. She cracks up at Whoopee cushions, Spongebob, and Tina Belcher on *Bob's Burgers*. She's also really good at doing voices, whether when reading children's books for kindergartners at my school or doing the voices of my stuffed animals. The funniest is Chewy, my goofy-faced Teddy Bear who takes everything literally.

"Hey, Chewy," I said on the night of my first practice. "This year we're gonna beat the pants off United Trust."

"I hope they're wearing clean underwear!" responded Mom in Chewy's toddler-like voice.

Me: "We're going to kill them!"

Chewy: "You'll go to jail!"

Me: "We'll hand them their lunch!"

Chewy: "Hot dogs or hamburgers?

Me: "We'll mop the floor with them."

Chewy: "Do you clean windows, too?"

Mom broke into laughter.

I went to bed that night musing about Morey's Funeral Home. Could our new coach, Mr. Quinn, turn us clowns around? Could I meet his expectations as a team leader? Could we unseat the great power, United Bank & Trust, and somehow win the league championship?

"Ya gotta believe," I whispered to Chewy.

"Believe what?" he replied.

Chapter 2
Nine Clowns I Call My Teammates

"You're not a real ballplayer," my dad once said, "until you have a nickname." I thought he was exaggerating until, one day, I looked it up. Seemingly every other guy in *The Baseball Encyclopedia* has a nickname. Some are simply silly and sing-songy. Major-league baseball has seen the likes of Yo-Yo Davalillo, Still Bill Hill, and Emil "Hill Billy" Bildilli.

In the old days, some nicknames touched on a player's ethnicity. Reliever Al "The Mad Hungarian" Hrabosky was a door-slamming relief pitcher in the 1970s. I can't tell you much about Lou "The Nervous Greek" Skizas except that he probably wasn't as relaxed as "Cool Papa" Bell. Other nicknames are pure poetry, such as "Blue Moon" Odom and "Sudden" Sam McDowell, whose fastball reached the plate in a hurry.

Some nicknames refer to a player's physical attributes. "Pee Wee" Butts, I'm guessing, had a tiny heiny. Nick "Old Tomato Face" Cullop may not have been the handsomest pitcher in the league. Other nicknames focused on players' habits or shortcomings. "Fidgety" Phil Collins didn't inspire confidence, nor did three-time 20-game loser Bill "Can't Win" Carrick. Moreover, teammates probably kept their distance from "Spittin'" Bill Doak.

Morey's Funeral Home had enough goofballs that it wasn't hard to tag them with nicknames. Featured below are personal profiles of every player on Morey's roster. Gary, Riley, and I came up with the nicknames.

Gary Smolenski
"Gas"

Gary's nickname had nothing to do with the amount of baked beans he consumed. (That was his own personal business!) It had everything to do with Pete Rose, baseball's career hits leader (4,256). Every now and then, Gary announced Rose's immortal line, "I'd walk through hell in a gasoline suit to play baseball." And you know what? He would.

Highly charged and wild-eyed, Gas channeled all of his energy into baseball. He grunted when he swung the bat and chased after fly balls in the outfield—even when he was playing shortstop. He was every teacher's nightmare, but every coach's dream-come-true.

Riley Dinkelberg
"Gutsy"

Riley was no Gold Glover at third base (his usual position), but he had incredible guts. On the last day of third grade, he ventured into the teachers' lounge—strictly off-limits to all students—and plunked 75 cents into the school's only pop machine. Mr. Clark abruptly whisked him out of the lounge and to the principal's office—but not before Riley cracked open and chugged an icy cold Mr. Pibbs. Riley has joked about it ever since. He jokes about everything, which makes him a good benchmate during those tense one-run games.

Jeffrey Quinn
"The Prince"

Riley and I called Jeff "The Prince" (though not to his face) because he possessed everything a kid could ask for. He had a massive TV in his bedroom, had been to Disney World four times, and owned a bat bag that was big enough to store his own personal catcher's equipment. Jeffrey had once been happy-go-lucky and fun to play with, but he gradually became more moody and snotty. Riley said he had become spoiled rotten. Jeffrey certainly was one of our better players, but I grew weary of his "country club" attitude.

Gus Voot
"Bu-bye"

Gus' nickname was like Steve "Bye-bye" Balboni's because he could belt the ball farther than anyone—at least anyone on our team. Gus swung a big bat but rarely said a word. My dad compared him to Tigers legend Charlie Gehringer: "He says hello on Opening Day, goodbye on Closing Day, and in between he bats .350."

However, my dad insists that Gus' name will prevent him from big-league stardom. "Gus Voot is not a baseball name," Dad said. "Reggie Jackson, Joe DiMaggio, Chipper Jones—those are baseball names. Simon and Garfunkel sang, 'Where have you gone, Joe DiMaggio?' What are you going to say: 'Where have you gone…*Gus Voot?*'"

That may be true. But if my team were down to its final at-bat and we were trailing by a run, the guy I'd want at the plate is Gus. "Bu-bye," we'd say as the ball disappeared into the great beyond.

Tashia
"Profanity Jane"

Every 10-year-old Little League team, it seems, has exactly one girl. For Morey's, Tashia was it. As Coach instructed, we were never to use the phrase "for a girl." You know: "For a girl, she can hit." I can respect that. But you know something? For a girl, she had a pretty foul mouth.

Tashia had long, curly dark-brown hair that she held back with one of those scrungy, rubbery things. If she muffed a groundball and someone laughed at her, Tashia would shout, "Go stick it up your nose, you little...." She'd always omit the last word, since profanity wasn't permitted on the baseball diamond.

Jackson Joseph
"Joseph Jackson"

Mrs. Whitaker was reviewing fractions with our class when she noticed Jackson staring out the window.

"Jackson, what are you doing?"

"I'm looking at a squirrel."

"You're looking at a squirrel during math class."

"He's squatting on a bird's nest eating a piece of toast."

"And why does that intrigue you?"

"Because he looks like he's on the toilet reading the *Wall Street Journal*."

At school or on the diamond, Jackson always had his head in the clouds. Once, when it came to his turn at bat, he was spotted at the ice cream truck ordering a melon slushy. Everything about Jackson was unpredictable. Even his name seemed backwards— hence his nickname.

Marty Gluckman
"Deadpan"

Marty's nickname came from his dour, deadpan expression. With his face perpetually locked in a frown, he spoke in a monotone voice and was always doom and gloom. "We're down 6-1," he'd say matter-of-factly. "We don't stand a chance. Might as well pack it in." Marty's saving grace was his glove work in left field. Otherwise, it was like teaming with Morey himself.

Evan Dixon
"Wonderbaby"

Everybody on our team was 10 years old. Except Evan. He was seven.

I first noticed Evan when he was a toddler. He was shorter than his bat, but when I tossed him balls, he smashed liners over my head. "How old are you?" I asked him. "I dunno," he said with a shrug.

Evan is too good to play with his peers, so his dad placed him in our league. Though he didn't have the arm to play third base or short, he made all the routine plays at second and could swat hits past diving infielders. If any Morey's player had big-league potential, it was Evan Dixon. Remember the name.

Rupa Kovner
"The Quiet Man"

Rupa and his mother, according to Tashia's sources, moved from Latvia to Michigan when he was a toddler. I don't know if he spoke Latvian, but he never learned English very well. By the time he reached preschool, he froze up whenever he was supposed to speak. It was painful to watch him talk, as he clenched his face and forced words out one at a time: "I...don't...want...milk...with that."

Though Rupa and his mother lived in a small townhouse in the worst part of Hickory Oak, he was bussed to that suburb's well-to-do Lovelton School so he could take special ed. The kids from Lovelton formed the United Bank & Trust team. That club had so many talented baseball players that Rupa didn't dare sign up to play. In fourth grade, he transferred to our school and joined Little League for the first time.

Rupa couldn't hit, and he could barely play catch. The one thing he could do, as Coach Quinn discussed, was run the bases. But that doesn't help you if you never reach base.

These were the eight boys and one girl who I went to war with every game. For three years, we had done nothing to make even our mothers proud. But under Coach Quinn, during this one magical season, we were about to make history. Together.

Chapter 3
Opening Day: All Things Are Possible

It was moments before our first game, and the team stirred anxiously on the bench. The exception was Tashia, who chatted casually on her phone.

"Go to YouTube," she instructed her friend while chomping on her Hubba Bubba. "Then search 'elephant that paints.'"

Gary, sitting next to Tashia, sighed in annoyance. He doesn't believe kids should bring a phone to the ball field. He thinks it disrespects the game. It's like bringing a yo-yo to church, he said, or a Slinky.

"Then try 'elephant...paintbrush,'" Tashia said. "He actually paints with a paintbrush, like on a canvas."

"That video's a fake," deadpanned Marty. "Computer-generated imagery."

"No, it's not," Tashia said.

Gary was really getting aggravated.

"No, the elephant doesn't *shove it up* his trunk," Tashia told her friend. "He holds it like a pencil."

Gary jumped to his feet. "Enough with the stupid elephant!"

"It's a hoax," Marty said.

"It's Opening Day!" Gary cried. "Don't you know what that means?"

"It means you're a jerk," Tashia said.

"It's the beginning of life!" Gary said. "Didn't you ever read the book *Why Time Begins on Opening Day?* We start anew. All things are possible."

"All right, guys," Coach Quinn interrupted. "We're in the field."

"Yes, sir!" said Riley.

And with that, we took to our positions. Jeffrey earned the nod as our Opening Day starter. He would pitch to Gus, our rock behind the plate. I manned first base, hoping that Riley could make the throws from third. I also wondered if Gary (shortstop) and Tashia (second base) could turn double plays better than they got along. Marty, Jackson, and Rupa manned the outfield. Evan, the Wonderbaby, would have to pay his dues on the bench this inning. He sat next to my dad, who deemed himself the best scorekeeper in Hickory Oak.

It was "a beautiful day for baseball," as Tigers announcer Ernie Harwell used to say. Warm sunshine illuminated the diamond on this Saturday morning, while a cool breeze kept us invigorated. "Hoo-yeah!" Gary cried.

We all looked sharp in our red and black jerseys (we looked like the Boston Red Sox). And for the first time ever, we believed in ourselves. Coach Quinn had been a master of preparation. He had schooled us on proper form—from batting and pitching to fielding grounders and flys. Practices were filled with "situations." "If you're on first and the batter singles to right, what do you do?" he asked. "Go to third!" we replied.

Now our epic season was about to unfold. "Play ball!" the umpire yelled.

A team called Wieners and Still Champions (named after a hot dog joint) was up first. Immediately, we flashed our hot leather. Riley gobbled up a Sunday hop and fired a strike to first base. Tashia turned a buzzing worm-burner into the second out. After Rupa dropped a fly ball for an error, Jackson made a circus catch in center. The high fly was hit right to him. The first thing he did—inexplicably—was throw off his sunglasses. Then he tossed his cap. Then he ran in, then back, then in again before making a "diving" catch. (It was actually more like a belly flop.)

Nothing Jackson did on the diamond made sense. He was like the legendary Yankees catcher Yogi Berra. Berra was short and squatty, yet he set a major-league record for most career home runs by a catcher. He consistently swung at pitches outside the strike zone, yet he hardly ever struck out.

Berra was known for his Yogi-isms—quotations that didn't make sense but yet kind of did. "It ain't over till it's over," he said. And: "It's getting late early." My dad's favorite is the one about the restaurant: "Nobody goes there anymore. It's too crowded."

While the parents overly applauded Jackson's catch, Gary focused his scorn on his right fielder. "Ya gotta catch those, Rupa. It was a can of corn."

"What…," Rupa managed to say, "is a…can of corn?"

"It's an easy flyball that's hit right to you," Gary said.

"Why do they call it a can of corn?" asked Evan.

"Because it…uhhh…."

The Gas-meister was stumped. But because it's meaningless history, my dad knew the answer.

"Back in the day," my dad began. He always opened stories with "back in the day." I still don't even know what that means. What's "the day"? Last Tuesday? Eight billion years ago? What?

"Back in the day," Dad said, "they had little mom-and-pop stores where you bought your groceries. The stores were small, so they installed lots of shelves, stacked toward the ceiling. If the owner needed to get a can of corn from the top shelf, he'd use a long stick to knock it down. He'd hold out his apron with both hands, and the can would fall softly and easily into the apron. It was…a can of corn."

"Wow…," said Evan, full of wonder.

On the mound, Jeffrey was mowin' 'em down. Through three innings, he had walked three Wieners, hit one in the rump, and punched out four (that means he struck them out; not slugged them in the face). He had yet to allow a run or a hit.

"Way to go, Bob Feller," Gary said.

"Rapid Robert" Feller of the Cleveland Indians is the only big-league pitcher ever to throw a no-hitter on Opening Day. On a frigid, windy afternoon in Chicago in 1940, he held the White Sox hitless.

"I bet you didn't know," Dad said, "that the Indians signed Feller for $1 and an autographed baseball. When he was 17, he tied a major-league record with 17 strikeouts in a game. Then, when the season was over, he went back to Iowa to finish high school."

"Nahhh…," said Jeffrey.

"Mr. Vehousky, you're just making that up," Jackson said.

"No, I'm serious," Dad said. "In fact, he was the only major-league pitcher to strike out his age until Kerry Wood fanned 20 for the Cubs in 1998."

"I'm going to strike out my age today," Jeffrey said. However, he never got the chance. Little League is like the Major League All-Star Game: Nobody pitches more than two or three innings. Gary, Riley, and Gus tossed an inning apiece. We had the Wieners playing "catch up" all day, and we cruised to a 9-4 win.

I did all right for myself: a pop single to center sandwiched between a walk and a groundout. But what impressed me was our professionalism. When Tashia caught a line drive to end the game, we didn't throw our gloves up in the air like a bunch of wild yahoos. We kept our cool. We congratulated the Wieners ("good game, good game, good game…"). And we even packed the equipment bag like Coach Quinn asked us to.

"That was great fundamental baseball," Coach said in his postgame pep talk. "You were aggressive at the plate, made smart decisions on the bases. Our pitchers threw strikes. How many walks did we give up today, Doug?"

"Uhhh…just six," said Dad, looking in his scorebook. "And as for hitting, every one of our hitters either got a base hit or put the ball in play."

"Not Rupa," Jackson blurted. "He struck out all three times."

"Jackson!" Coach Quinn shot back. "Don't be dissing your teammates! Go run to the right field fence and back."

"That's not very far," Jackson said.

"Then do it twice!" Coach demanded.

As Dad reviewed the scorebook, realizing his mistake, our normally cheery coach gave us a stern warning.

"Now I told you kids every day in practice about treating people with respect," Coach Quinn said. "Riley, who do we respect?"

"Our opponents, our coaches, the umpires…*and*…our teammates," Riley said.

"And during the week…Gus?" Coach asked.

"Our parents and our teachers," Gus said.

"That's right," Coach said. "Okay, now you played a great game today and I'll see you at practice on Tuesday at 5:30."

Coach looked up and saw Jackson climbing the right-field fence and running into the distance.

"Where is he going?" Coach asked.

"Home, probably," Jeffrey said. "He lives across the street."

"Well, he's gonna be batting 10th in the order next game—I tell you that," Coach said.

"But I won't be here," Riley said.

"Then ninth then!" Coach said.

I packed my bat bag and walked off the field with my dad. All of us left with our parents except Rupa, who sat slumped over on the bench. As Dad and I walked to the parking lot, we noticed Coach Quinn taking a seat next to Rupa.

"Man, I feel terrible," Dad said. "I can't believe I didn't see that in the scorebook."

"Maybe he just needs more time in the batting cages," I said.

"That would help," Dad said. "But hitting is a lot about self-confidence—believing in yourself when you're at the plate."

Back on the bench, Coach was still sitting with Rupa, giving him cheer-up pats on the back. You almost knew what he was telling him: "At least you went down swinging. Keep your chin up. We've got a long season ahead."

The whole scene was strange because Jeffrey stood nearby with his arms folded. Rupa doesn't have a dad around, and Coach was acting like he was *his* dad. And yet Coach just got divorced, so Jeffrey doesn't see him half the time.

"Does Rupa hang out with you guys at recess?" Dad asked.

"Uhm, he usually just kind of wanders around the edges of the playground," I said. "He has this bouncy ball that he bounces—it kind of gives him something to do."

"A bouncy ball?"

"Yeah, like one of those super rubbery balls that bounce real high."

As we reached Dad's Malibu, Rupa's mother pulled up and got out of her car.

"Good morning," Dad said.

"Good morning," she said in her Latvian accent. "How did the game go?"

"Oh, real well," Dad said. "We won 9-4."

"Wonderful!" she said. "How did Rupa do?"

"Oh…he played real well," Dad said. "I think he's still over there with the coach."

"Oh, okay. Thank you!"

We got in the car and put our belts on. Dad sighed and started the engine. We drove amid a long, awkward silence. It's strange how, when we're alone together in the car, we never have anything to talk about. Sometimes, the silence becomes unbearable.

"So who's pitching for the Tigers today?" Dad asked, finally breaking the silence.

"Fullmer," I said.

"Excellent."

That was the extent of our conversation until we pulled into our driveway. Mom was planting flowers but got up to greet us. It was nice to see her smiling face.

Chapter 4
Pitcher's Off His Rocker! He Throws Like Betty Crocker!

The next Saturday, I was scheduled to start our game against Curl Up and Dye Salon. Gary came over at 9 A.M. to help me warm up. For some reason, I couldn't find the strike zone.

"All right, three-one count," Gary said as he squatted for my next pitch. "Just throw to the glove."

I threw it five feet over Gary's head. This wasn't like me. But with game time looming, I was tighter than a clenched fist.

"Dude, you've got to loosen up," Gary advised. "Have fun with it. The umpire says 'play ball'—not 'work ball.'"

Gary was right. I had to relax, have fun with it. I started to think about Bill Veeck, the old owner of the American League's St. Louis Browns. He spent his career trying to make baseball fun for fans. Veeck was the guy who signed Eddie Gaedel to a one-game contract in 1951. Eddie was a little person, standing only 3'7". In a game against Detroit that summer, Gaedel emerged from the dugout in a Browns uniform. The little guy carried a miniature bat in his hands and was headed for home plate.

"What the heck?" muttered the home plate umpire. Gaedel, wearing the uniform number 1/8, stepped into the batter's box. To further shrink his strike zone, he bent into a crouch.

"Keep it low," catcher Bob Swift advised his pitcher. Bob Cain threw four straight pitches out of the strike zone to Gaedel, who trotted proudly to first base. "For a minute," Eddie said, "I felt like Babe Ruth."

Yeah, have fun with it. In the minor leagues, that's what the games are all about. A lot of teams have goofy mascots. My favorite is Uncle Slam of the Potomac Nationals. In the minors, the promotions are even crazier than Veeck's. One of them was called Two Dead Fat Guys Night. It was staged on August 16, the date on which both Babe Ruth and Elvis Presley had died. Another team held Star Wars Night. Stormtroopers played the National Anthem, and Darth Vader threw out the first pitch.

Keep it fun, I said to myself as I stood on the mound that Saturday afternoon against Curl Up and Dye. But I couldn't convince myself. I was as nervous as "Jittery" Joe Berry, the old reliever for the Philadelphia A's. With each pitch, I kept asking myself, *When should I release the ball?* You can't think that way. Ya gotta just "let it happen."

I walked three of the first four batters I faced. I glanced at the dugout, where Dad buried his head in the scorebook. He was writing down "BB"—not for Barry Bonds, but for Base on Balls. In the bleachers, Mom sat in agony, looking as if I was undergoing open-heart surgery. Sensing my nerves, Gary came in from shortstop to calm me down.

"So, uh, Jacob," he said. "How did the pig get to the hospital?"

"What?"

"The pig. How did he get to the hospital?"

"Huh?"

"In a *ham*bulance," he said. "Get it?"

"What are you talking about?"

"I'm trying to loosen you up with a joke. That's what you're supposed to do when the pitcher is struggling."

It didn't help. I gave up four runs that inning on four walks and a double. "Pitcher's off his rocker!" one of their guys shouted. "He throws like Betty Crocker!" When I returned to the dugout, none of the kids talked to me. They weren't mad at me, but what do you say to someone who screwed up so badly? Dad thought he had the answer.

"Every good pitcher has a rough outing," he said.

"It was my *only* outing," I shot back.

Our team would have been better off if I had stayed home. We lost the game 5-4. It was all my fault.

"Whenever *I'm* feeling upset," Dad said after the game, "I like to take a drive downtown."

That's Dad for ya. What better way to cheer up than drive through the most rundown city in America? But several hours after the game, Mom, Dad, and I sat on a bench overlooking the Detroit River. The smell of car fumes was in the air.

Sixty years ago—back in the day—Detroit was a thriving city of nearly two million people. But over time, most people moved to the suburbs. Houses and stores were boarded up, and crime became rampant. Now, more people live in Mississauga, Ontario, than Detroit.

"I like watching the boats float down the river," Dad said as he and Mom ate Chinese food.

"It seems like half the boats are trying to escape Detroit to the north," I said, "and the other half are trying to flee to the south."

"Nah, the city's coming back," Dad replied. "Next week we'll visit Midtown."

"Jacob, don't you want some lemon chicken?" Mom asked. "It's like McNuggets."

"No, I'm not hungry."

Dark clouds were gathering in the distance, reflecting my mood. *I can't believe I screwed up so badly,* I thought to myself. *I'll never pitch again.*

I used to dream of being the next Satchel Paige. He was the Negro League legend who won 2,000 games and tossed 55 no-hitters. Paige's repertoire included a dozen pitches, and he gave them all nicknames. My favorites were the Bat Dodger, the Two-Hump Blooper, the Four-Day Creeper (his change-up), and the Barber. The Barber, legend has it, would shave the hairs off the batter's chin.

"At least I didn't stink at the plate," I said.

"Jacob!" Mom said. She put her arm around my shoulder. "You're a great player. Why are you so hard on yourself?"

"Ah, that's just the nature of the game, Bridget," Dad said. "You're supposed to feel bad after each loss."

"So when the Tigers went 43-119 in 2003," I asked, "they felt lousy practically every day?"

"Pretty much," Dad said. "But three years later they were in the World Series."

That's true. In baseball, you always get another chance. In Game 2 of the 1956 World Series, Yankees pitcher Don Larsen stunk up the ballpark. But in Game 5, he pitched a perfect game. Ya gotta believe—in your team and in yourself.

"So Dad, what was like the greatest moment you ever saw—like in person or on TV?"

"Uhm, probably when Henry Aaron broke Babe Ruth's home run record." He looked off into the distance and rubbed his chin. "I remember it well...."

"Oh brother, here we go," Mom said, rolling her eyes.

"I was in my GI Joe jammies, the ones with the fuzzy feet. It was a Monday night in April, and my parents told me to go to bed. 'Let me see him bat just once more!' I begged. Aaron had grown up poor in Alabama. His arms were strong from picking cotton in the fields, and he practiced his hitting by swatting bottle caps with sticks."

Dad loved telling stories. There was no stopping him.

"Aaron started out in the Negro Leagues with the Indianapolis Clowns," he said. "Some of the restaurants didn't like serving the team because the players were African American. At one restaurant in

Washington, D.C., the workers smashed all the dishes because the black players had eaten off them."

"Doug, this doesn't have to be a history lesson," Mom said.

"He's got to know this stuff, Bridget. Anyway, by '74 Aaron had tied the great Babe Ruth with 714 home runs. And as I watched on ABC's *Monday Night Baseball,* he socked No. 715 off Al Downing at home in Atlanta. I'll never forget his mother running out on the field and giving him this huge hug when he crossed the plate. It's also my favorite radio call of all time: 'There's a new home run champion of all time, and it's Henry Aaron!'"

I had heard that before on an MLB commercial. When I was in second grade, I used to go to bed at night saying, 'There's a new home run champion of all time, and it's Jacob Vehousky!'"

The Aaron story made me think of some of the other great moments in history. One I wasn't sure about.

"What was the Mad Dash?" I asked.

"Slaughter's Mad Dash?"

"Uh-huh."

"It was the seventh game of the 1946 World Series, Red Sox versus the Cardinals in St. Louis," Dad began. "The score was tied 3-3, with two outs in the bottom of the eighth. Enos "Country" Slaughter was on first when the manager called for a hit-and-run. Slaughter took off while Harry "The Hat" Walker lined a single to left-center."

"So then Slaughter dashed all the way to third?" I asked.

"Yes, but he didn't stop. He rounded third and headed home!"

"On a single?"

"Yes! The shortstop, Johnny Pesky, held the ball for a while. It hadn't occurred to him that Slaughter would even consider running home. By the time Pesky threw to the catcher, Slaughter slid in safely. The Cardinals won 4-3."

"Now *that*," Dad concluded, "is aggressive baseball."

Late that night, I looked up a photo of the Mad Dash in my *Baseball Chronicle.* Slaughter glided like a plane into home plate, his hands tilted up, a puffy ball of dust behind him. It was an elegant finish to a daring dash.

That's the kind of attitude I needed to bring to the next game, I told myself.

Vehousky's Mad Dash. That's what they'll call it.

Chapter 5
Tuesday with Rupa

"Don't look back," Satchel Paige used to say. "Something might be gaining on you."

That's how I felt going into our third game. I had put my pitching disaster behind me. Now it was full-steam ahead.

"Come on, Morey's!" I blared, rattling the dugout fence before the game. "Let's get some runs!"

"Mor-eys! Mor-eys! Mor-eys!" the guys chanted.

With Wednesday's contest rained out, we were playing a rare Friday game. We had no homework and no bedtime, and everyone was on a sugar high. It was Evan's eighth birthday, and his mom had brought cupcakes with each of our numbers on them. They were supposed to be for after the game. But once Jackson opened the Tupperware lid, it was a mad free-for-all.

Excitement was in the air at Hickory Park, and I led off the second inning with a sharp single to center. I proceeded to kick first base a couple inches toward second.

"What are ya doing there, Jake?" asked Coach Quinn, who coached first base.

"It's a trick I learned from Ty Cobb," I said.

Cobb, who played a hundred years ago, was the greatest Tiger of all. He holds the major-league record for career batting average (.366). But he was a mean son-of-a-gun. One time, he went into the stands and beat up a fan. When someone pointed out that the poor guy had no hands, Cobb said, "I don't care if he's got no feet!" When kids wrote letters to him, he threw them into the fireplace. "Saves on firewood," he would mutter.

Like Enos Slaughter, Cobb was a madman on the bases—and so was I. On the first pitch, I took off in an attempted steal of second. Riley swung and ripped a single to right, and I kept on going—all the way around third base!

"Whoa!" Mr. Majus said, raising his arms to stop me. I slowed up and returned to third. "You don't take risks like that when there's nobody out," he said.

No gambles were necessary in this game. We defeated Snooze at Eleven (the mattress store) 8-3. The bottom of the order came through for us. The birthday boy cracked two singles, Tashia blooped a double, and Jackson got hit by the pitch *three* times. Rupa mustered a walk along with his three strikeouts.

The next morning, we won 5-4 over Dr. Aiken Family Dentistry. That nail-biter lasted nine innings, three more than the normal limit. Jeffrey had to leave in the eighth to go to Travel Team soccer practice.

"Oooh, I guess he's too good for us," Tashia said, as Jeffrey's mom drove him away in her Mercedes.

When the game entered the ninth, it sparked a discussion of the longest games in baseball history. "I saw the Mets play 18 innings once," said Gus, a native New Yorker.

"The record…," Rupa said, "is…33 innings."

He was right. Back in 1981, the Red Sox of Pawtucket, Rhode Island, hosted the Rochester Red Wings in a minor-league game. The 1,740 fans who attended the Holy Saturday game saw two future Hall of Famers—Wade Boggs of the Red Sox and Cal Ripken of the Red Wings.

In the 32nd inning, at 4:00 A.M., they were still playing. By that time, only 19 fans remained. It was freezing, with the wind chill temperature in the 20s. Pitcher Bob Ojeda gathered up all the broken bats, threw them into a big trash can, and lit them on fire to keep warm. They played the 33rd inning the next day, and Ripken's team finally won. By that time, they had played eight hours and 25 minutes, thrown 882 pitches, and used 156 baseballs. "I got four hits," Boggs told his dad, "but I was up 12 times." Dallas Williams had perhaps the worst game ever. He went 0-for-13.

Our Marty was no Dallas Williams. In the bottom of the ninth, he smoked a line single to left, scoring Gus from third with the winning run. Even then, Marty didn't crack a smile.

"Another day at the office," he said as he strode back to the jubilant bench.

In his postgame game speech, Coach Quinn praised Marty for displaying "mental toughness in a pressure situation." He awarded him the game ball. One thing I've noticed in Little League is that coaches love to award game balls to the lousy players. I guess they're trying to spark their confidence. However, it's annoying because a great player could go like 5-for-5 and pitch a no-hitter and not get the game ball.

"I bet that by the end of the season," Riley told me afterward, "you, Gus, Gary, and Jeffrey won't have any game balls and Marty, Jackson, and Rupa will have like a dozen of them."

"Yeah, really," I said.

"Well," he added, meanly, "maybe not Rupa."

With a record of 3-1, we were feeling pretty good about ourselves. But now we entered the toughest part of our schedule. Coming up were Hickory Oak Proctologists and We Will Wok You Chinese Family Buffet.

The Proctologists were really good. Their starting pitcher shut us down for three innings while they mounted a 4-0 lead. We held little hope as we prepared to bat in the top of the fourth.

"What's a proctologist?" Evan asked.

"Butt doctor," Marty replied instantaneously. It's like Marty couldn't wait for someone to ask that question. It's like he had been saying it in his head the whole game: *butt doctor, butt doctor, butt doctor.*

"Why do you need a butt doctor?" Jackson asked.

"Oh, for heaven's sakes!" Gary said. "Let's concentrate on the fact that we're getting our butts *kicked*!"

"Come on guys," Coach Quinn encouraged. "Focus. We can beat this team."

But we couldn't. After Tashia pitched the fifth inning and got rocked, we trailed 8-1. As we returned to the bench, Gary sighed and threw down his mitt.

"What's your problem?" Tashia asked him.

"Girls can't pitch," he said.

"Hey, you shut the…," Tashia said, charging at him.

Luckily, the coaches were on the field and didn't hear them.

"Don't start!" big Gus said, glowering at Gary and Tashia.

"Not long ago," Tashia said calmly to Gary, "there was an 11-year-old girl from New York who threw a perfect game in Little League."

"Yeah, yeah, yeah…," Gary said.

"And it wasn't just a perfect game," she said. "She struck out *every single boy she faced!* Now her jersey's in the Baseball Hall of Fame. So don't give me this 'girls can't pitch' crap."

Riley started to dance and sing: "Go Tashia…go Tashia!"

"And how about Jackie Mitchell?" said Dad as he walked in on the discussion. "She faced the New York Yankees in an exhibition game and struck out Babe Ruth and Lou Gehrig back to back."

"Well, we could use Jackie Mitchell right now," Gary said, "because we're getting skunked."

We lost the game 9-2, then dropped the Saturday game as well. Amidst a steady drizzle at Hickory Park, We Will Wok You walked all over us, 6-4. Coach Quinn's decision to move up Rupa to the sixth spot of the batting order backfired. Jeffrey, who batted third, singled and walked. Gus, the cleanup man, smashed a double and two singles. I batted fifth and mustered two singles and a walk. Yet Rupa kept stranding us on base by striking out *four* times. Nobody said what everyone knew: Rupa blew the game.

In Coach's postgame speech, Rupa sat at the end of the bench with his head down. His face was smoldering, but through great effort he succeeded in holding back his tears. Afterward, he walked toward the parking lot. He couldn't even bear to greet his mother, or even look at her. She wrapped her arm around his shoulder, and they walked away together.

Three days later, Mrs. Kovner dropped off Rupa at our house. This was *not* my idea, but my mom's and dad's. "Jacob, your coach had asked you to be a team leader," Mom had said. "This is your chance."

The truth is that Mom had felt sorry for Rupa and thought that someone should invite him over to play. The "leader" thing was just an excuse.

"Hi, Rupa!" Mom said as he and Mrs. Kovner arrived at the door.

"Hi, Mrs....Vou...Vou...."

"Thanks so much for inviting Rupa," his mother said.

"Oh, it's my pleasure!" said Mom, going overboard with the sweetness. "We've been talking about getting the boys together for a while."

Riley was supposed to come to help ease the tension. But he weaseled out of it with a lame excuse: "Uh, I have to accompany my mother to go wax the car."

"Hey," I said to Rupa.

"Hi," he said.

"You want to…go to the basement?" I asked.

I led him down the steps. Our basement is big but unfinished. The floor is bare concrete, and the walls are smooth cement. I pulled the long string that turns on the light bulb, revealing our shelves of board games.

"Anything look good to you?" I asked.

Amid Star Wars Monopoly and Battleball, Rupa found his game of choice. He pointed to Connect Four.

This is the game in which you drop plastic "checkers" down slots. You try to get four in a row of your color. It's like tic-tac-toe, but much brainier. Since I was family champ at this game, I figured I could mop the floor with Rupa. *I'll have to take it easy on him,* I thought to myself.

We set up the game on the table in the dining room, a cramped little area outside the kitchen. As

Rupa and I dropped checkers, I realized that the kid could play. He had the concentration level of a mad scientist. He beat me in the first game…and the second, third, and fourth.

"Man, where did you learn to play like this?" I asked.

He mustered a half-smile.

"I'm…good at games," he struggled to say. "I'm very good at…at…at…chess."

"You play chess?" I asked.

"Yes. I…usually beat my uncle…. And when he was…in school…he was…chess champion."

I started to think about what my mom had said. "Everyone's got strengths and weaknesses," she told me. "Your father pulled straight As in school, but he has no sense of direction when he drives. Your Aunt Renee speaks four languages, but she can't remember a thing. Albert Einstein was dyslexic, as was Thomas Edison. Babe Ruth ate too many hot dogs, but he could hit the ball a mile."

Rupa had trouble speaking, but he had a brilliant mind. He beat me in the fifth game with moves I had never seen before.

"Whoa!" I said, as he broke into a smile. I was totally impressed.

Rupa and I played baseball in the basement. One of us would throw the tennis ball off the wall, and the other would hit it with a Wiffle bat. A liner off the wall was a single. If you hit it above certain lines, it was a double, triple, or home run. I let Rupa be the Tigers while I was the Yankees. I won the game 14-13, but it took me 10 innings. And we smashed only one light bulb.

Afterward we watched *The Simpsons,* the one where Homer gets a job as Mr. Plow. Rupa stayed for dinner (Mom's homemade mac and cheese, with breadcrumbs), and then his mom came to pick him up.

The dreaded "play date" with Rupa turned out to be pretty fun. I wish I could say the same for our next game.

Chapter 6
Slaughtered by United Bank & Trust

"I feel like jolly ol' England," Gary said, "right before the Germans dropped the bombs."

It was 10 minutes before game time at Hickory Park, and eight of us sat shivering on the bench. It wasn't just the chilly Saturday morning air that had us shaking in our cleats, but the team we were about to face. Our opponent was United Bank & Trust, the most talented, wealthy, spoiled, and dominating team Hickory Oak Little League had ever seen.

While Jeffrey warmed up with Gus behind our bench, the rest of us watched the spectacle unfold in front of us. Coach Jonathan K. Reynolds hit groundballs to his infielders. "Turn two," the coach said. "Why, Dad?" asked his second baseman/son, who flawlessly executed the play. "They'll never get a guy on first base." The coach chuckled to himself. "Be a good sport, Morgan," he said.

In the outfield, another coach swatted high fly balls, which fell softly into the players' gloves. Behind the backstop, a third coach tossed balls to a menacing hitter, who drilled liner after liner into the fence. We cringed every time the ball crashed into the chain-linked metal. *Smash!... Smash!... Smash!... Smash!*

"It's psychological warfare," Riley said. "They're trying to rattle our brains."

"Don't let 'em get to you guys," said Coach Quinn, whose expression was filled with worry.

United Bank & Trust was no ordinary team. They had won the seven-, eight-, and nine-year-old Hickory Oak championships and were gunning for their fourth straight title. Jeffrey said they had never lost a game.

"There's something not fair about this," Tashia said. And there wasn't. Mr. Reynolds, an executive with United Bank & Trust, wasn't just the team's coach. He was the commissioner of the entire Hickory Oak Little League! Dad had been grumbling about that for three years.

"If you're the umpire, and the *commissioner* comes out and argues the call, what are you going to say?" Dad said. "You're going to say, 'Yes, sir, Mr. Commissioner. I'll reverse my call right away, Mr. Commissioner. Please don't fire me, Mr. Commissioner.'"

Coach Reynolds, with his slicked-back hair and confident posture, oozed wealth. In fact, all of UB&T's players were from the wealthy Lovelton School. While our moms and dads sat on the bleachers, their parents brought their own foldout chairs—with double cup holders.

Jeffrey was the only Morey's player to play Travel League ball, a summer league that you have to try out for. Almost every UB&T player, if not all of them, played Travel ball. Jeffrey said that most of them worked out at Frozen Ropes. That place is really expensive, but the kids get instruction from professional ballplayers—some of whom played in the major leagues.

Even their uniforms were a cut above. While our jerseys were just T-shirts, they wore button-down jerseys like the pros wear. UB&T's uniforms were all white except for their team name on the left side of their jerseys. It was written in fancy blue script: United Bank & Trust. Not only that, but they were the only team to have their names on the backs of their jerseys.

Everyone called UB&T the Bankees, and not just because they were named after a bank. They were rich and powerful, like the New York Yankees.

"All right, guys," Coach Quinn said. "Let's give it our best shot. What's our motto?"

"Ya gotta believe," Evan said.

"I believe we're doomed," said Marty.

Before we took the field, my dad showed me the Bankees' lineup card. The other scorekeeper had written down each of the players' current batting averages. The highest was .667. The lowest was .385. Everyone else was batting in the .400s or .500s.

"I can't believe he wrote down their averages," Dad said.

"Is he trying to intimidate us?" I asked.

"I don't know," Dad said.

I was still shivering when we took the field. Jeffrey, our ace pitcher, was firing strikes during warm-ups. But when the umpire yelled "play ball," Coach Reynolds came out to cause problems.

"Blue," the coach said. (In baseball, coaches call the umpire *Blue.*) "The pitcher can't wear a jacket under his jersey."

While Coach Quinn frowned, the ump made Jeffrey remove his jacket. He returned to the mound wearing a white, long-sleeved Under Armour shirt beneath his jersey.

"The long sleeves have to go, too," Coach Reynolds told the ump.

"What?" said Coach Quinn, running onto the field.

"It's in the rules, Pete," Coach Reynolds said. "Pitchers can't wear long, white sleeves. It distracts the hitter."

"But your team's uniforms are *completely* white," Coach Quinn said.

"But we don't wear long sleeves. It's in the rules."

"Well, who wrote the rules?" Coach Quinn said in frustration. Coach Reynolds probably did. He's the commissioner.

Jeffrey took off his Under Armour, leaving him with just his uniform T-shirt.

"Jon, it's 45 degrees," Coach Quinn said. "I don't want these kids catching colds."

"It's all right, Dad," Jeffrey said.

"Your son can wear his white sleeves, or his jacket, if he plays another position," Coach Reynolds explained. "Just not on the mound."

Gary, fuming at shortstop, couldn't hold back. "You're just trying to take our best pitcher out of the game," he said.

"Hey!" Coach Reynolds retorted while walking toward Gary. "Do you want to play another game in this league?"

"Yes," Gary shot back.

"Then I suggest you shut your mouth!"

"I'll take care of my players," my coach told Mr. Reynolds.

"Well, I think you should take this shortstop of yours out of the game as punishment for mouthing off."

"Well…I'm not going to do that," Coach Quinn said.

Coach Reynolds snickered and shook his head, and both coaches returned to the dugouts.

"All right, guys," Coach Quinn said with a sigh. "Let's have fun."

Now freezing on the mound, Jeffrey struggled to get the ball over the plate. The leadoff man walked, stole second, stole third, and came home on a wild pitch. Somehow, Jeffrey got out of the first inning trailing only 2-0.

Gary returned to the dugout with fire in his eyes. "At least Coach Quinn stood up to that coach," Gary said. "Now it's payback time."

The Bankees' pitcher was firing bullets, but Gary rifled a line-shot single on the very first pitch. "Yeahhh!" we cried from the dugout. But when he tried to steal on the next pitch, their catcher gunned him down.

As Gary trotted back to the bench, the catcher took off his mask and glowered at him. "That'll teach ya to open your mouth," he told Gary. The catcher was a big, massive kid. The name on his jersey said Sludowski. He had a real ticked-off expression, and he followed Gary with angry eyes until Gas reached our dugout.

"What's *his* problem?" Tashia asked.

"That's…Sludowski," Rupa said. "But they call him…Sludge…. I…hate him."

The look on Rupa's face revealed that he truly disdained that kid. He later told me that Sludge had teased him for three long years. A lot of the kids at Lovelton School (the UB&T kids) had made fun of Rupa, but Sludge was the biggest bully. "When you try to talk, your face looks like it's constipated," Sludge had told him.

They were mean, horrible words. Rupa, I'm sure, had revenge on his mind when he stepped into the batter's box in the third inning. "Hey, Rupa," I could hear Sludge say. "Do you hit as well as you talk?" The kid was cruel.

Rupa took a mighty swing on the first pitch, but missed. Sludge smiled. "Don't be afraid to throw inside," he told his pitcher. The next pitch was indeed inside, causing Rupa to jump back. "Strike!" boomed the umpire. Down 0-2, Rupa took the next pitch down the middle. He retreated to the dugout. "At least swing at it!" Sludge scolded.

I would have expected Rupa to throw his helmet or something. But he merely sat on the end of the bench, by himself. I guess if you kick a dog for so long, it loses its will to fight. Rupa looked defeated. "You'll get 'em next time," Jackson told him.

But there wouldn't be a next time. While Jeffrey deserved a Cy Young Award for allowing just five runs in three innings to the Bankees, Riley didn't fare as well. While pitching the fourth inning, he coughed up five runs of his own. After we went down one-two-three in the bottom of the fourth, the score was 10-0. That was it. In Little League, if you're up by 10 runs after four innings, the game is over. Some refer to it as the mercy rule. Others call it the slaughter rule. Each applied. UB&T showed no mercy, and we were slaughtered.

"Well, at least you weren't the 2007 Baltimore Orioles," Dad told the team. "They lost one game to Texas 30-3."

"Doug," Mom said over the fence. She put her fingers to her lips and made a "zip it" gesture, as if to say *the kids don't want to hear that now.* We were all pretty down.

"It's okay, guys," Coach Quinn said, as we took our seats on the bench. "Nobody ever beats this team." The coach couldn't think of anything else to say. "Did you at least have fun out there?"

"Uh, it was like freezing, and we got killed," Riley said. "So not really."

"Why are they going back on the field?" Evan asked.

The Bankees were about to scrimmage amongst themselves.

"They win every game by slaughter," Jeffrey said. "So they play a practice game afterward to get more innings in."

Coach Quinn stared at the Bankees and then looked at his own team—a long row of dejected faces. Gary sighed. Evan's feet dangled back and forth.

"Tell you what," he told us. "Let's have an extra practice tomorrow, where we concentrate solely on hitting. The proper stance, the swing, the weight shift—the whole ball of wax. And then afterwards, if it's okay with your parents, I'll take you all to Buddy's for pizza."

"Buddy's!" Jackson blurted.

Buddy's is *only* the best pizza in Michigan.

"No. 1, *Detroit News*," Marty blurted. "No. 1, *Detroit Free Press*."

Buddy's pizza comes in thick, square slices with cheese that oozes over the sides. I like mine with mushrooms.

Evan turned toward his mother. "Can I go, Mom?" he asked. "Can I go?" His mom and some of the other parents smiled and nodded yes.

"All right then," Coach said. "Practice and pizza. Now let's hear it."

We stood and put our hands together.

"One, two, three," Coach said.

"Ya gotta believe!" we cried.

After that morning's game, we didn't yet believe we could win the league championship. But we believed in Coach Quinn, and that was a good place to start.

Chapter 7
The Bugs Bunny Change-Up and a Lesson About Perfection

Thanks to Coach Quinn's Sunday hitting clinic, Morey's Funeral Home was digging a grave for Little Miss Muffin. By the fourth inning of this sunny Wednesday road game, we were beating the bakery-sponsored team 6-4. With runners on first and second and nobody out, I had a chance to bust the game open. What followed was the craziest hit in Morey's history.

Coach had taught me how to drive my hips forward when I swung. This, he said, would generate more power. Against the Muffin left-hander, I blasted a high fly to deep right-center. The center fielder caught it on the run and rolled on the ground, but then the ball popped out of his glove. The skinny teenage umpire froze, not knowing whether to call it a catch or a hit.

Poor Mr. Majus was unsure what to do with his three baserunners. At first he sent Riley and Gus back, thinking the outfielder had caught the ball. But when the right fielder threw the ball to the infield, he waved them along. I had thought that the kid had dropped the ball, so I tried for a triple. The result? Three guys standing on third base!

"This can't be good," Riley said.

The third baseman took the ball and tapped all three of our helmets. I looked around, and everyone was cracking up.

"Two of you have to be out," the ump shouted.

"Which two?" asked Mr. Majus.

"I have no idea, sir."

Gus, the upstanding teammate, volunteered to leave. But if I left, I'd be credited with a double instead of a triple. So Riley and I did rock, paper, scissors. He won. I trotted off amid cheers and chuckles.

"Did that ever happen in the major leagues—with three guys on one base?" Evan asked my dad.

"Just once," he said. "Brooklyn Dodgers, 1926. Don't ask me how it happened."

The play launched a discussion of the strangest hits in baseball history. Dad remembered when a fly ball bounced off outfielder Jose Canseco's head and over the fence for a home run. No one could top that.

We wound up beating Little Miss Muffin 10-5. We were now 4-4 with four games left to go. The hitting clinic had worked out so well that Coach Quinn added a baserunning workout for Sunday, May 23, and a fielding clinic for May 30. Since the parents determined that we shouldn't eat at Buddy's *every* Sunday, Riley's and Marty's parents hosted post-practice get-togethers on those two days.

Coach Quinn worked wonders in those practices. Jackson learned how to slide for real instead of just plopping on his butt. The infielders learned how to stay really low on groundballs. "It's much easier to field a chopper when the ball's bouncing at eye level," explained the former college infielder.

The other kids and I became closer during those last two weeks—better teammates, better friends. With wins in our next two games, we improved to 6-4. It felt good to know that for the first time in Morey's history, we wouldn't finish with a losing record. Even Dad got into the winning spirit. "If you kids win the championship," he said, "I'll take you all to Farrell's for ice cream."

"Can we order The Zoo?" Jackson asked. The Zoo is a massive ice cream creation that serves more than 10 people and costs $50. It's 30 scoops of ice cream topped with whipped cream, cherries, almonds, pecans, and bananas. Two waiters are needed to lug the monstrosity to the table.

"Absolutely," Dad said. "It'll be on me."

You have to know that my Dad isn't a big "splurge" guy. He's so cheap that when his underwear gets too tight, he snips the waistband with scissors rather than buy a new pair. I'm sure he was also thinking that winning the championship would be impossible as long as United Bank & Trust was in the league.

Nevertheless, we enjoyed our success while it lasted. I was on a tear at the plate, upping my average to nearly .400. Noting my sky-high confidence, Coach Quinn put me in to pitch against Drain Surgeons in Game 10. Since we were leading 8-2 in the fifth, it was no big deal. I retired all three hitters for a "Lawrence Welk," as Gary referred to it.

"What," Gus asked after the inning, "is a Lawrence Welk?"

"It's a one-two-three inning," Gary explained. "You know that old bandleader who was on TV? He'd begin each song with 'and a one, and a two, and a three….' It's on my list of best baseball lingo. Here…."

Gary pulled a crumpled piece of paper out of his pocket. He had printed out an article entitled "Best of the Best Baseball Lingo." The list included:

Bugs Bunny changeup: A pitch that seems to stop in front of the plate—similar to what Bugs Bunny threw in his cartoons.

Five o'clock hitter: A player who hits great during five o'clock batting practice but stinks during the game.

Go full gorilla: To give 100-percent effort.

Golden sombrero: Going 0-for-4 with four strikeouts.

Lawrence Welk: A one-two-three inning.

Linda Ronstadt fastball: It blew by you (named after Ronstadt's famous song, "Blue Bayou").

Mendoza Line: A .200 batting average. Named after shortstop Mario Mendoza, who always struggled to hit over .200.

No room at the inn; bags are juiced; ducks on the pond: All terms that mean that the bases are loaded.

Reagan-era fastball: Thrown in the mid-80s.

Uncle Charlie: A big-breaking curveball.

"My favorite," Gary beamed, "is go full gorilla!"

"I like the Bugs Bunny changeup," Jackson said. "I want to throw one of those."

I actually tossed a Bugs Bunny in the season finale. We had lost our 11th game 8-7 to Sew What?, but we mopped the floor with Oodles of Poodles Dog Grooming in our last game. I pitched the fifth inning of a 10-2 blowout, allowing a single but no walks or runs. My Bugs Bunny actually worked. The super-slow-mo pitch dropped to the ground right before the ball reached home plate. The hitter swung and missed for strike three. "Bubba-da-be-ba, da-be-ba, da-be-ba," Riley said. "That's all folks!"

What I most remember about that day was coming home with my dad and turning on ESPN. "Oh, my gosh!" Dad screamed. "No!... No, no, no!"

Mom came running into the living room, panicked. "What happened?" she asked, figuring that some building had blown up.

"Lopez pitched a perfect game, but the umpire blew it!" Dad said.

"That's what you're screaming about?" Mom asked.

"Look at this!" Dad said, pointing frantically to an instant replay of the Tigers-Twins game at Comerica Park. "It's an outrage!"

Ricardo Lopez, a lanky right-hander out of Cuba, had retired the first 26 batters he had faced. He was just one out away from a perfect game, which means no hits, no walks, and no baserunners allowed. No Tiger pitcher had ever thrown a perfect game, and there had been only 23 in major-league history. Now Lopez was on the brink.

On the 27th batter, the count went to 1-2. On the next pitch, he fired a fastball that was *definitely* in the strike zone. The batter waited for the umpire to call him out on strikes, but he never did. On the next pitch, the batter stroked a single.

"Look at the replay: It was in the middle of the strike zone!" Dad blared. Dad's face was beet red. Steam was practically coming out of his ears. "How could he make such a stupid call when a perfect game was on the line…. He should be fired!"

"Doug, calm down," Mom scolded.

"I'm serious, Bridget. That umpire blew it. He blew it for everybody."

A lot of people in Detroit were as angry as my dad…until they heard Lopez in an interview later that night. The pitcher had talked to the umpire, who had admitted that he had blown the call. Lopez didn't feel sorry for himself. He felt sorry for the umpire.

"I mean, he feels really bad," Lopez said. "He talked to me and he said, 'I don't know what to say to you. I'm really sorry.' You know, he feels really bad. I said, 'I'll give you a couple of hugs.' And I said, 'Nobody's perfect.'"

The next day, Lopez handed the lineup car to the umpire before the game. The ump, who gave the pitcher a pat on the shoulder, had tears in his eyes. So did my dad, who told me he was sorry for his angry outburst.

"Well," Mom said, "I think we learned a little lesson about baseball. It's not always about being perfect and beating the heck out of the other team. It's about good sportsmanship and doing the right thing."

Those were lessons that Coach Quinn had taught us well. In more ways than one, it had been the best regular season in Morey's history.

Now it was time for the playoffs.

Chapter 8
"Storming" Through the Playoffs

"There's baseball," Coach Quinn told us, "and there's *playoff* baseball. They are not the same thing."

It was an hour before our first playoff game, and the team sat attentively on the bench at Hickory Park. On this Saturday afternoon, we were focused and ready for battle against Dr. Aiken Family Dentistry. We had earned the home field advantage over Dr. Aiken due to a better record (7-5 versus 6-6). But if you recall, Dr. Aiken had taken us to extra innings during the regular season.

"We can't wait for Marty to get the big hit again," Coach said, cracking a smile. "We need to be aggressive early. When you're at bat, focus hard on every pitch. When you're in the field, think about the situation. How many outs are there? What base should you throw to if the ball is hit to you?"

"Use your head," Coach continued, tapping his temple. "And play with heart."

The school year had ended the day before, so we could concentrate exclusively on this game. The only distraction would be the wind, which howled across the diamond. I could just picture Jackson chasing his cap around center field while the batter ripped a hit up the middle.

"All right, guys," Coach said. "Let's warm up."

Everyone ran to the field except Jeffrey. He sat glumly on the bench twirling a baseball in his hand.

"Jeffrey," Coach said, but no response. "Jeffrey!"

Jeffrey jumped up in a huff, threw the ball into the dirt, and stormed out of the dugout.

"Is he all right?" I heard Dad ask as I played catch with Rupa.

Coach didn't know how to answer. "He's been having a lot of trouble with the divorce," he finally said.

"Ah," Dad said. "He has seemed kind of quiet this year."

Coach nodded. "And now his mother is taking the kids to her family's place in Kansas for the summer. So after the playoffs, I won't see them until August."

I glanced at Coach Quinn. His normally cheery expression had drained out of him. He looked sad, and older, as he watched Jeffrey play catch in the infield. Then he snapped out of it.

"Okay, let's go!" Coach said as he grabbed a bat and trotted toward the plate. "Ya gotta believe, right guys?"

In this game, all I believed in was the power of Mother Nature. The wind blew harder and harder as the innings progressed. Pitches fluttered around like knuckleballs, leading to a game of walks and strikeouts. By the fourth inning, I had walked twice in two trips. Hats were flying off everyone's head—not just Jackson's. Evan's little brother served as the cap retriever, running onto the field to retrieve errant headwear.

"Hey, Blue," Tashia said to the umpire. "Can you call a game on the count of wind?"

The ump, an older guy with a bushy mustache, took off his mask. "You can call it 'cause of rain, you can call it 'cause of snow," he said. "You can call it 'cause of darkness and lightnin'. But you can't call it 'cause of wind…unless there's a tornado."

Riley and I scanned the skies for a twister, but to no avail.

"The good news," Gary shouted amidst the bellowing wind, "is that it's blowing toward center field. If someone could hit a fly ball, it'll sail to Kalamazoo."

By the bottom of the fifth, storm clouds had gathered on the horizon. The score was still tied at 6-6, and we had two outs and nobody on. Gus swung and missed on a flutterball, going to 0-2 in the count. A few drops of rain began to fall, and my dad turned his back to the field to address the team.

"I hope you guys score next inning," he yelled, "because the rain won't hold out any longer than…"

Before he could finish his sentence, we jumped off the bench to what sounded like gunfire. With a mighty swing, Gus crushed the ball high and deep to center field.

"That's outta here!" Tashia screamed.

"Bu-bye!" Gary cried.

Caught in the wind stream, the ball flew and flew and flew—well beyond the outfield fence. "Whoa! Yeah!" we screamed. It was the longest blast since Reggie Jackson rocketed a pitch into the Tiger Stadium light tower in the 1971 All-Star Game. (Or so it seemed!) We rushed toward home plate to greet the big fella, who cracked a rare smile.

As the rain picked up, we hurried to complete the top of the sixth. With three quick outs, we could go home with a victory. "I don't need any stinkin' warm-ups," Gary said as he took the mound. "Let's go."

Firing one strike after the other, Gary made quick work of Dr. Aiken. He fanned the first man, got the second to ground out to Evan at second, and got the third to pop one up. "I got it!" cried Riley at third base. But the ball kept carrying and carrying—all the way to left field, where Marty made a hard play look easy.

"Can o'corn," he said as he trotted in after the game-ending catch.

We had no time to celebrate. For as soon as we slapped skin with the other team, rain gushed from the heavens. We all made a mad dash to the parking lot. When Mom, Dad, and I got home, we were drenched.

"It was raining cats and dogs, Chewy!" I said.

"Schnauzers or Weimaraners?" Chewy asked. "I bet there were lots of poodles in the puddles."

I had little time to let my first playoff victory soak in. The next afternoon, we arrived at a soggy Hickory Park for the league semifinal game. Our opponent? Curl Up and Dye. They had finished just 5-7, but they had beaten us on the day of my horrid pitching performance. Moreover, they had pulled off a playoff shocker against Hickory Oak Proctologists, which had gone 9-3 during the season. Since we had a better record than Curl Up and Dye, we again got to play at home.

"If we win this game," Riley said as we arrived at the park, "we'll get the chance to lose to United Bank & Trust."

"Maybe they'll lose *their* semifinal game," Evan said, naively.

"They never lose," Marty said.

Getting to the title game wouldn't be easy due to Curl Up's starting pitcher. A tall kid with long, flowing, blond hair, he pumped bullet after bullet over the plate. Gary was just as nasty, striking out six in three innings.

The tension mounted in the later innings. Like soldiers on the front lines, we were on high alert with each pitch. Gus pitched well in the fourth inning. But in the fifth, he allowed the game's first run on a two-out wild pitch. Now we trailed 1-0. As Yogi Berra said, it was getting late early.

"I'll get us even," Gary said as he led off the bottom of the fifth. Sure enough, Gas came through again. He lined a single to left, stole second, and stole third. "Nobody out," he shouted from third. "Bring me home, guys."

Boy, that kid loved the big games. He was like Reggie Jackson, who hit three home runs in Game 6 of the 1977 World Series. Reggie was so good in the postseason that they called him Mr. October. "We're gonna have to call Gary Mr. June," I told my dad.

Gary did score, but no thanks to us. Their fifth-inning pitcher, a small boy with a ponytail and a worried look on his face, crumbled under the pressure. He walked Tashia and Jeffrey to load the bases. Gus grounded out to first, scoring Gary to make it 1-1. With runners on second and third and one out, I had the chance to be a hero. But I walked too, loading the bases.

Their coach tried another pitcher, but he was just as nervous. He walked Evan, forcing in the go-ahead run. Three more walks pushed us up to five runs, the maximum allowed in a Little League inning. The 5-1 lead made me feel at ease, but I didn't feel like we were earning our spot in the championship game. It felt like they were giving it to us.

"This is too much pressure to put on the shoulders of 10-year-olds," Dad told Coach Quinn. "Especially pitchers."

Even with a four-run cushion, Gus had a hard time closing it out. He walked two and struck out two before facing the ponytail boy.

Gus blew away the poor kid on three pitches. Curl Up and Dye was dead. Morey's Funeral Home was off to the championship game.

While our parents gave us a standing ovation, we were strangely subdued as we gathered in the dugout. We eagerly packed the equipment, perhaps knowing it was the last easy thing we would have to do that season.

"Maybe the Bankees lost," said Evan, still dreaming.

"I just heard," Riley's dad said. "They won 10-1. Slaughter rule."

Coach Quinn didn't say much during his postgame speech. "I just want you all to know," he said, "that whatever happens on Friday, I'm extremely proud of you guys. You were willing to learn, you worked hard, and you got better every week. I'll see you all at practice on Tuesday. 'Morey's' on three."

We put our hands together. "One, two, three— Morey's," we said.

Jackson tapped me and whispered, "Why didn't we say, 'Ya gotta believe'?" I shrugged, although I sensed that Coach didn't believe we could beat UB&T. I didn't either. In fact, those words *whatever happens on Friday* gave me a cold chill. Ten to one. Slaughter rule. We were in for it.

Coach called Dad and me aside.

"Say listen," he said, addressing mostly me. "Because of the playoff rules, Gary and Gus can't pitch more than one inning on Friday. So Jacob, I'd like you to start the game and give us an inning or two. What do you say?"

My whole body went numb. Start in the championship game...against the Bankees? Was Hell booked for the weekend?

"Maybe...their coach won't know that Gary and Gus pitched three innings," I said.

"No," Coach said with a laugh. "Believe me: He'll know. Come on, I need you. You pitched great those two games."

"Yeah, but that was mop-up duty in a couple of blowouts," I said.

"Jake...I need you, buddy. I don't have anyone else. Just one inning."

I nodded. I didn't know what else to do.

That afternoon, the Tigers got trounced by the Kansas City Royals 7-2. I couldn't have cared less. I had to start against United Bank & Trust. And I had five days to fret about it.

Chapter 9
The Mad Dash

It was 4 P.M. on Friday, and I sat alone on the living room couch. The grandfather clock ticked and tocked like a time bomb. My countdown was to eight o'clock, when I would take the mound against United Bank & Trust.

The week had felt like an eternity, and this day was pure torture. Who would schedule a championship game five full days after the semifinal game—and then not start it until eight o'clock? I was convinced that Coach Reynolds had concocted the whole plot. *Let 'em worry themselves sick the whole week,* he undoubtedly schemed. *By Friday night, they'll be putty in my hands. Ah ha ha ha ha ha ha ha!*

"Jacob," my mom called from the kitchen. "Your food is ready."

I lumbered to the kitchen for my last meal. My mom had made all my favorites: a bowl of cream of wheat (which she called porridge); a glass of cranberry juice; sliced strawberries topped with sugar; and two slices of cinnamon toast, one with jelly and the other with peanut butter.

"Thank you," I said as I slumped into the chair. "But I don't think I can eat all this."

"Just eat what you can, honey," she said. "And when you're done, I want you to have this."

She plopped a bottle of Pepto-Bismol on the table. She knew I was a wreck.

At 6:45, I sat in the Malibu's back seat with my uniform on, feeling like I was six years old. Dad was standing outside Rupa's townhouse door, waiting for him to come out.

"He's saying he doesn't want to go," his mom said. "I think he's nervous."

"I think the whole team has a case of Bankee-itis," Dad said.

Both went inside the townhouse. About 10 minutes later, they emerged with a uniformed Rupa. We rode in the back together, barely saying a word.

We arrived at Pleasant Park, where the Hickory Oak travel teams played their games. The ball field dominated the little park, which was surrounded by nice homes. I had never played on a diamond this beautiful. The infield was perfectly groomed, and an electric scoreboard stood behind the center field fence.

We would play under the lights, something Morey's had never done.

"I better warm you up, Jake," Dad said.

As players from both teams started to arrive, Dad and I ran to the diamond. I pitched to him from the mound, trying to get in as many throws as possible.

"I know you can throw harder than that," Dad said. "Rear back and fire it."

I tried, but I couldn't generate any velocity. My arm felt like a wet noodle. Did you ever have a nightmare in which you tried to run but you kept going in slow motion? It was like that, only with my arm.

Coach Reynolds looked at me and snapped his fingers three times. "We got the field," he demanded.

I went back to the bench on the third base side. Because we had won a coin toss earlier in the week, we were the home team. While some of our guys nervously unpacked the equipment, Marty watched the Bankees take infield practice.

"We're doomed," he said

"Shut up, Marty!" Jeffrey retorted. "I'm sick of that schitck."

The tension was unbearable—for all of us. Out on the field, we saw Coach Quinn talking with Coach Reynolds. Our coach was clearly upset about something. We understood why when he pointed to a tall, broad-shoulder player on the Bankees—a kid we had never seen before. The name on his uniform said Hulse.

"He's 11 years old," Coach explained when he returned to the bench. "But since he didn't turn eleven until after June 1, he's eligible to play in our league."

"What?" Tashia said.

"He's eligible," Coach said, "and they signed him…so…."

"That's bogus," Gary said.

We all thought it was bogus. As if they didn't have enough star players, they had to sign the "Incredible Hulse," as Riley called him.

Being the championship game, the league went all out. They had two umpires instead of one, and they played the national anthem on a boom box. A crowd of at least 60 people—including grandparents, aunts, and uncles—stood with us. Our team mostly hummed the National Anthem, but Gary knew all the words.

"All right, Morey's," Coach Quinn said. "Let's play our best."

I ran to the mound and warmed up with Gus. I forced myself to throw harder, but my pitches were all over the place. I noticed that the skinny teenage ump was behind the plate. Coach Reynolds probably picked him, I was certain, because he knew he could intimidate him.

"Play ball!" the ump cried.

I looked up to see the Incredible Hulse step into the box. *Why were they doing this to me?* I said to myself. My first pitch sailed over the umpire's head. I grooved the next pitch, and the kid unloaded. The ball shot like a missile over my head and kept on going. Jackson, the center fielder, turned around and saw the ball bang off the top railing of the metal fence. It hit so hard, I thought the whole structure was going to collapse. Hulse cruised around second and slid in with a triple.

At that moment, I felt short of breath. I hunched over and put my hands on my knees. My head was spinning.

"Are you okay?" I heard people ask.

Soon I felt a large hand on my shoulder. "I'm okay, Coach," I mustered.

"It's Dad."

My dad had never taken the field during a game, until now.

"Just take some breaths," he said, rubbing my back. "If you need to come out, we'll take you out."

I stood up straight and took some deep breaths. I saw my mom standing on the bleachers and looking concerned. "Just take your time," Dad said.

"We need to move it along, Coach," Mr. Reynolds barked from the dugout. "If you're gonna take him out, then take him out."

Boy, that coach got on my nerves. Suddenly, I felt a surge of determination rush through my body.

"I'm staying in," I said.

"All right!" Dad said, with a final pat. "Go get 'em, Jake!"

"Yeah!" cried Gary, as the parents applauded. "Just let 'em hit it, buddy. We got you covered—right, guys?"

"Let 'em hit it, Jake," Riley said, pounding his glove from third.

"We got ya, Jacob," Tashia said.

Behind the plate, Gus nodded and pumped his fist.

"Ya gotta believe," Jackson shouted from center field.

The ump allowed me a couple warm-up tosses, and I fired my best fastballs over the plate. The next batter cracked a hard one-hopper to Gary's left, but he snared the ball and nailed the runner at first. Although a run scored, we cheered Gary's big-league play.

"I told you we got ya," Gary told me.

I got the next guy, the infamous Sludge, to pop out to Jeffrey at first. With the count 1-2 on the next hitter, Gus set up high. I fired an eye-level heater, and he swung and missed. "All right!" my team cried, and I ran to the bench amid a flurry of high-fives.

"You want to go another inning?" asked a fired-up Coach Quinn.

"Yeah, I think so," I said.

Playing under the lights, on a warm spring night, was exhilarating. Across the street, high school seniors had gathered at a graduation party. I could smell the burgers on the grill, and music filled the air. It was turning into a magical evening.

I survived the second inning thanks to a lineout double play and a groundout to Jeffrey. "You're pitching one more inning," said Coach Quinn with a smile, "whether ya like it or not!"

Though we still trailed 1-0, I was soaring when I took the mound in the third. The kids at the party were playing the famous Chumbawamba song: "I get knocked down, but I get up again. You're never going to keep me down." I fired strike after strike as I sang the lyrics in my head. Strike out. Single. Stolen base. Groundout to Gary. And finally, a sky-high popup in the middle of the diamond. "I got it!" I screamed at the top of my lungs. I caught the ball, and then skipped off the field amid backslaps and a standing ovation from Morey's moms and dads.

"Let's get some runs!" I yelled, practically jumping out of my shoes.

The drama escalated in the bottom of the third. With two outs, Rupa batted for the first time. "Move in, guys," the catcher, Sludge, yelled to his teammates. "Closer," he said. The fielders, now grinning, moved in even closer. Rupa, fuming inside, took the first pitch for a strike.

"I told you last game," Sludge said, "*swing the bat*."

"Shut up!" Rupa blurted.

Sludge stood up and stared Rupa down before the ump intervened. Coach Reynolds ran onto the field. "Blue, that's grounds for ejection," he said.

"You want me to eject him?" the ump said, as if asking for permission.

Realizing that UB&T was better off with Rupa *in* the game, Coach Reynolds shook his head. "But son, you better watch your mouth, because that behavior isn't tolerated in this league."

"I'll take care of my players, Jon," Coach Quinn shouted from first base. Rupa's mother, sitting next to my mom in the bleachers, was visibly upset.

Play resumed, and Rupa ended up drawing a walk. As he got a lead, the pitcher threw to first. Rupa was safe, but then the first baseman tagged him out with the hidden-ball trick. "Ha!" Sludge cackled. Rupa walked back to the bench, humiliated.

"Don't worry about it," I told Rupa. "We're gonna win this game for you."

By the fourth inning, the teenagers at the party had learned of the drama on the diamond. David was facing Goliath in the championship game, and he was trailing only 1-0. At least a dozen of them came over to watch—and root for Morey's Funeral Home.

With one out in the top of the fourth, Jackson made the defensive play of the game. With a man on third, Gary yielded a high fly to short center. Jackson caught the ball. Then, as the runner tagged and ran home, he rifled a perfect throw to the plate. The runner avoided Gus's tag and then reached back to touch the plate. "Safe!" the ump exclaimed.

It looked like we were down 2-0, but Coach Quinn ran onto the field. "No, no, no!" Coach insisted. "The runner cannot touch the plate with his hand." He turned to Coach Reynolds. "It's in the rules."

"The coach is right," the umpire said. "The batter's out!"

"Woo-hoo!" we screamed.

Coach Quinn had beaten Coach Reynolds at his own game—a rulebook technicality. "Way to go, Coach!" Riley exclaimed.

We didn't score in the bottom of the fourth, but Gus shut down their hitters in the fifth. Incredibly, we tied the game at 1-1 in the bottom of the inning—thanks to Gary. He ripped a single, stole second, and went to third on a wild pitch. When Gus grounded to short, Gary came home easily.

"Yeah!" he yelled as he high-fived each of us with a vengeance. "Yeah! Yeah! Yeah! Yeah!"

The score remained 1-1 in the top of the sixth—the last scheduled inning. More partiers, and others from the neighborhood, came to see if history would be made. My mom and Mrs. Kovner sat anxiously in the bleachers. Someone cranked the music higher. "I'll Stand by You," by the Pretenders, inspired us to stay strong.

Jeffrey took the mound. "We need your A game, Jeff," Coach said. Unfortunately, in the biggest moment of his life—on the day before he left for Kansas—Jeffrey couldn't get it done. Of the first five hitters he faced, he struck out two but walked three. Jeffrey then faced Sludge with the bases loaded…and he walked him on four pitches. The next hitter ended the inning with a pop-out to Gary, but the damage had been done. We trailed 2-1.

Jeffrey walked off the field with his head down and sat on the end of the bench. He buried his face in his hands, and soon I saw tears roll down his fingers. Coach sat down next to him.

"It's okay, Jeff," Coach said.

"I let everybody down," Jeffrey cried. "Everybody...."

"No, no," his dad said. He wrapped his son in his arms, and Jeffrey cried like a baby. "It's not you," his dad said. "It's not you.... Come here."

Coach led his son away. In the distance, he and Jeffrey's mom tried to comfort him. "I think," my dad said to me, "that this is about more than just baseball."

I barely noticed that the bottom of the sixth had begun. Jackson, always unpredictable, surprised everybody with a bunt. It was a beauty, and their third base man had no chance at throwing out Jackson. "He's the tying run, guys," Gary announced. "We can tie this thing!"

Or so we thought. Coach Reynolds brought in the Incredible Hulse to pitch. Our jaws dropped to the ground as he fired smoke into Sludge's mitt.

"Oh...my god," Tashia said.

"You can't hit what you can't see," Riley said.

"Okay, Evan," my dad said. "You're up."

The little guy lugged his bat to the plate. Three pitches later, he lugged it back to the bench. Tashia was next. She swung and missed on the first two pitches, but the second one got past the catcher, allowing Jackson to go to second. On the next pitch, she swung and missed. Two outs.

It was all up to the last man in the order, Rupa. I expected he'd be a quivering mess when he walked to the plate. But a calm had come over him. I could see the concentration on his face, like when he beat me at Connect Four.

"The best pitcher in the league against the worst hitter in the world," I could hear Sludge say. "I wonder how *this* is gonna turn out."

On the next pitch, Rupa lined a hard foul to the right side. "Yeah!" we cried. "Way to get a piece of it!"

For the next pitch, Sludge set up way inside. "You want a shot at glory…," he told Rupa before the next pitch drilled him in the arm, "…but you're not going to get it."

Rupa writhed in pain on the ground as Coach came to attend to him. Amid sympathy applause, he got up and trotted to first.

"Blue," Coach told the umpire while pointing to Sludge, "if this kid opens his mouth once more, I want him out of this game."

With two outs and men on first and second, a red-eyed Jeffrey Quinn stepped to the plate. "Did you notice," my dad told me, "that they're playing songs for us." I hadn't realized it, but the kids at the party had been selecting inspirational songs: "The Climb" by Miley Cyrus, "Dream On" by Aerosmith, and now "With a Little Luck" by Paul McCartney & Wings.

Jeffrey swung and missed on the first pitch, then took two balls. Hulse reared back and fired a strike on the corner, making the count 2-2. By this point, everyone was on their feet. Jeffrey swung and fouled one back.

"Too much tension," Dad said. Gary was in the on-deck circle biting his knuckles. My mom was clinging to Mrs. Kovner's arm. *Swing and another foul.* Jeffrey's mom knelt by herself on the grass, her hands clenched. My knees were quivering, and I felt my heart racing.

What happened next seemed to play out in slow motion—like a magical dream. Jeffrey swung and swatted a short fly ball to right field. "There is no end to what we can do together," McCartney sang. "There is no end." The ball hooked toward the line but landed fair. Jeffrey scored on the single to tie the score, and Rupa headed for third.

But he didn't stop.

Coach Majus, the old man who had been *that* close to achieving his big-league dream so many years ago, waved his arm frantically like a windmill. "He's gonna wave him in!" Gary screamed. Their second baseman held the ball, not knowing what was going on. "Throw it home!" Coach Reynolds shrieked, his eyes bulging. "Throw it home!"

Rupa cut the corner perfectly at third and turned on the afterburners. He blazed toward home plate, his eyes afire. Like the legendary Enos Slaughter, Rupa was attempting his own Mad Dash!

Sludge caught the ball on one bounce and blocked Rupa's path to the plate. But Rupa threw it into overdrive and freight-trained into his nemesis. He knocked Sludge on his butt and busted the ball out of his glove. Rupa also fell to the ground. But as Sludge crawled and scrambled for the ball, Rupa got up and stepped on the plate.

Coach Reynolds ran at the umpire like a maniac. "The run doesn't count!" he screamed to the ump in a knowing lie. "Run doesn't count! Runner interference!" But the young ump was not intimidated. "The catcher was blocking the plate," the ump pronounced. "Runner is safe. Game over!"

"Yeahhhhh!!!!!" we screamed, jumping to the heavens. I had told Rupa we would win it for him, but *he* had won it for *us*! We mobbed Rupa at home plate while our parents and fans went wild. We had achieved the impossible dream: We had beaten the Bankees!

Like Hank Aaron's mom, Mrs. Kovner ran onto the field and hugged and hugged and hugged her son. Jeffrey, the other hero, grinned from ear to ear while bear-hugging his dad. Then, Coach Quinn picked up Rupa by the waist and hoisted him like a championship trophy. "You did it, Rupa!" Coach exclaimed, shaking him skyward. "You did it!"

Parents on both sides applauded and cheered. Rupa, pumping his fists in well-deserved pride, lit up the sky with his beaming smile.

During the trophy presentation, we all got to bask in the spotlight. Yet on this magical night, one more miracle remained: Dad pulled out his wallet. Making good on his promise, he treated all the kids to Farrell's ice cream. The guys and I gathered around The Zoo for one last team photo. It was, and probably will be, the greatest day of my life.

That night, I didn't get to bed until after 12. Mom and Dad said goodnight and then turned off the lights.

"Dad," I asked before he left the room, "why do you think Mr. Majus waved home Rupa on a single?"

"Well," Dad said, "he probably thought that with two outs, it was worth the gamble—especially with a tough pitcher on the mound."

I nodded.

"Then again," he added, "maybe he thought that *everyone* deserves a chance to be a hero."

Dad left, and I picked up my bear, who looked back at me with that goofy smile. He was holding an envelope. I opened it and read the short note:

We always believe in you.
—Chewy

Thank you for reading The Mad Dash!

If you loved the book, please leave a review. I'd love to hear from you!

Sign up for the latest info on upcoming books, bonus content, and giveaways at twistedkeypublishing.com

Made in the USA
San Bernardino,
CA